D0394331
2019
NO LONGER PROPERTY OF
SEATTLE PUBLIC LIBRARY

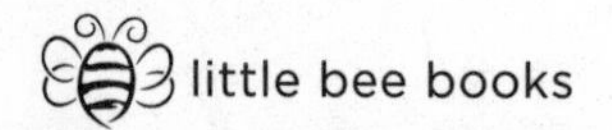

An imprint of Bonnier Publishing USA
251 Park Avenue South, New York, NY 10010

Library of Congress Cataloging-in-Publication Data is available upon request.

Printed in the United States of America LAK 1217
ISBN 978-1-4998-0611-3 (hc)
First Edition 10 9 8 7 6 5 4 3 2 1
ISBN 978-1-4998-0610-6 (pb)
First Edition 10 9 8 7 6 5 4 3 2 1
littlebeebooks.com
bonnierpublishingusa.com

by
Jaden Kent

illustrated by
Iryna Bodnaruk

TABLE OF CONTENTS

1

A MINOR DETOUR

"According to this map, the Lollipop Forest is this way," Owen said to his twin sister, pointing to his left as they flew toward home. "And way over there is the Evil Pumpkin Patch. And way, way over there where all the steam is? That's Goblin University, and we're *not* going there."

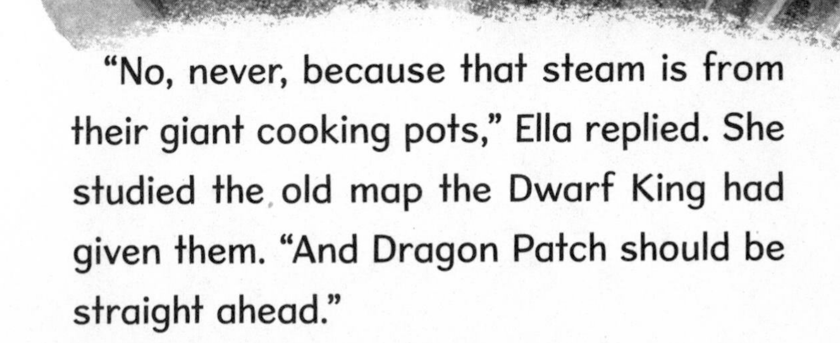

"No, never, because that steam is from their giant cooking pots," Ella replied. She studied the old map the Dwarf King had given them. "And Dragon Patch should be straight ahead."

Ella and Owen had brought peace to the conflict between the angry dwarves and the excitable elves, and a map showing the dragons how to get back home to Dragon Patch was their reward.

Their wings fluttered rapidly as they flew through the trees.

Owen snatched up the map. "I think Dragon Patch is that way, through the Valley of Stones that Look Like Faces," Owen said excitedly. "We're finally going home, and I'm going to go straight to my room."

"What's so great about your room?" Ella asked.

"Two things," said Owen. "First, it's where all my books are, and I've missed them. And second, it's not *your* room."

"That's because my room is super-dragon awesome, and—wait, did you hear that?" Ella paused to listen.

“No, I totally did not hear anything that sounds like two creatures arguing in the distance,” Owen replied.

“Let’s go check it out,” Ella said.

Owen pointed in the direction they were flying. “But that way leads to my room and my books!” he said. He pointed off in the opposite direction. “And do you know where the other direction leads? To arguing voices.”

“Being in your room’s even more boring than cleaning the beetle scum from my claws,” Ella said. “At least this might be something fun!” She changed direction and flew toward the forest to check out the voices.

“I know I’m gonna regret this.” Owen sighed and flew after his sister.

The voices grew louder as the dragons approached a clearing in the forest.

"Are too!" a boy's voice said.

"Are not!" a girl's voice disagreed.

When they got to the clearing, Ella and Owen could see who was arguing. Owen's eyes widened. His jaw dropped open.

"Unicorns!" he excitedly squealed. "They've even got unicorn horns and everything!"

“Uh, yeah.” Ella yawned. “If they had *two* horns, they’d be called ‘two-nicorns.’”

And they weren’t just unicorns, but *twin* unicorns. Their coats were iridescent and they had beautiful, flowing tails and manes. One unicorn had a shiny gold horn, and the other had a purple horn with sparkles. They appeared to be about the same age as Ella and Owen.

"I've never seen a unicorn before!" Owen said.

"So amazing," Ella said before pausing. "Are we sure they're friendly?"

"Let's go talk to them!" Owen then had a better idea. "Oooo! Maybe they'll let us ride them!"

Owen happily scampered toward the unicorns.

"I know I'm gonna regret this." Ella sighed and flew after her brother.

2
UNICORN TROUBLE

"I've always wanted to meet a unicorn!" An excited Owen fluttered toward the two bickering creatures. "Hey, who are you guys?"

Owen startled the two unicorns, but at least that made them stop arguing.

"Um . . . I'm Glitter Star," the first unicorn said. "And this is my twin sistercorn."

"Sparkle Pop," the second unicorn said. "We just saved Prince Twinkleberry Sunshine from an angry nest of razzle-dazzle jelly bees."

"And now we're on our way home," Glitter Star said.

"Us too!" Owen said. "Did you get lost? We're experts at getting lost. Mostly because I let my sister lead the way."

"Nope, we never get lost," Glitter Star said. "The Lollipop Forest is way over there and I always use my unicorn sense to get us back home."

“Right . . . unicorn sense.” Sparkle Pop snorted.

“But if you’re not lost, why are you arguing?” Owen asked.

“Oh, that!” Sparkle Pop replied. “We’re arguing because my brothercorn claimed that boy unicorns are better and more unicorny than girl unicorns.

“It’s not wrong if it’s true,” Glitter Star said.

"It's not true," Sparkle Pop replied. "Go ask any winged horse or fairy! Everyone knows that girl unicorns are better and more unicorny than the boys."

Sparkle Pop looked at Owen. "Which do *you* think are better?"

"Whichever one gives me a ride!" Owen said hopefully.

"Ignore my brother," Ella said. "He has scales for brains. It's clear to me that girl *and* boy unicorns are both awesome."

"Yeah!" Owen agreed. "From the tips of your tails to the tops of your unihorns!"

The unicorns looked at each other and smiled.

"After all, it's not like you're dragons," Ella added. "*Everyone* knows girl dragons are better than boy dragons. Just ask any griffin."

"Yeah!" Owen agreed, then snapped a look at Ella. "Wait, what?! Girl dragons are *not* better than boy dragons! Boy dragons are so much better!"

"Oh, hardly," Ella replied. "Your scales are too scaly and your fire breath is more like a hot sneeze."

"Well, didn't *you* get us lost in Terror Swamp earlier?" Owen said. "And chased by knights and captured by trolls and a Cyclops and some crazy elves and some even crazier dwarves and a talking pumpkin?!"

"Nope. That was all you," Ella replied.

"Oh no, it wasn't!" Owen argued. "Boy dragons are so much better than girly-girl dragons! My fangs are sharper and my wings are, uh, more *wingy*!"

"Girl dragons are better!"

"And girl unicorns are better than boy unicorns," Sparkle Pop resumed her argument with Glitter Star.

"Boy unicorns are better," Glitter Star replied.

"Just like boy dragons are better," Owen added.

"Girl dragons!" Ella said.

"Girl unicorns!"

"Boy unicorns!"

"Boy dragons!"

"Girl dragons!"

The four paused to catch their breath and then said at the same time, "CONTEST!"

3
ON YOUR MARKS! GET SET! GROSS!

"Everyone knows a contest is the only way to tell who's the best and who's a boy," Ella said to the group.

"Owen and I will pick the first challenge," Glitter Star said.

"And the first challenge will be to see who gives the best unicorn rides!" Owen said.

"No rides." Sparkle Pop rolled her eyes.

"It was worth a try," Owen said with a sigh. "Ooo! But first we need to have a cool name for our team, like . . . Team Dynamic Dragicorn!"

"More like Team Dynamic Lame-icorn." Ella laughed. "We're going to call ourselves the Winners, and leave it at that."

“I’ll pick our first girls vs. boys challenge,” Glitter Star declared. “Let’s see which team can collect . . . THE MOST GROSS SLUGS!”

“Ew, gross,” said Sparkle Pop and Ella. They both groaned.

“I love gross slugs! Who knew I had so much in common with a unicorn?” Owen let out a joyful sigh.

Owen knew three great things about gross slugs:

1. Gross slugs are truly quite gross.

2. They smell like the unwashed feet of an old, wrinkly troll.

3. They make gross noises that sound like swamp toads with tummy trouble.

"Go, Team Dynamic Dragicorn!" Owen yelled. Thoughts of icky gross slugs made him so happy.

Glitter Star and Owen ran to a nearby creek and jumped into the cold water with a big splash. A shiver ran up Owen's scales from the tip of his pointed tail to the tops of his pointed ears.

"I forgot that gross slugs love the cold!" Owen said.

"Grab as many as you can!" Glitter Star yelled.

Ella and Sparkle Pop crept up slowly to the edge of the creek.

"I hate gross slugs," Glitter Star said. "They're soooo . . . gross!"

"Here's one," Ella picked up a gross slug between her claws, then shook it off. "Argh! It's too gross to touch!"

The slug flew through the air.

It stuck to the scales on Owen's back. "Got one! Thanks, Sis!" he said.

Glitter Star jumped into the water, splashing like a water sprite on the first day of spring.

"Attention, gross slugs! Come out, come out, wherever you are!" he squealed. A gross slug splashed out of the water and landed on Glitter Star's back. "Got another one!"

Owen tucked himself into a ball and jumped into the water. "Dragonball!" he yelled as he flew through the air. A giant stream of water splashed up and showered right down on top of him. A gross slug dropped onto the end of Owen's snout. "Got another one too!"

Sparkle Pop sniffed at a rock in the mud. She rolled it over. There was a gross slug underneath.

"I'm sorry, but that one's just too gross!" Sparkle Pop kicked it with one of her hooves. The gross slug flew into the air and landed on top of Ella's head.

Ella squinched her face. "Ah, gross! It's sticking to me." She shook her head so hard her scales rattled. The slug flew off and landed right on the end of her long tail. Ella flicked her tail in disgust, sending the slug airborne.

Owen jumped and tried to grab it. He missed and plopped into the muddy bank of the creek and into a mess of even more gross slugs. The slugs splattered onto Glitter Star's face. Unable to see, he crashed into Sparkle Pop.

"Watch out!" Sparkle Pop fell against the bank and into another pile of gross slugs, which splattered onto Owen and stuck against his scaly skin.

Owen looked at all the slugs on his body and smiled. "Glitter Star! I've got like a jillion gross slugs!" he proudly announced.

Glitter Star turned his head. His body was covered in gross slugs too. "I've got a jillion more!"

"So, how did you girls do?" Owen asked.

Sparkle Pop's whole body shook. She raised her head into the air and sneezed. A gross slug flew out of her left nostril and landed at Ella's feet.

“I got one,” Sparkle Pop said. “One really gross, horrible, awful, slimy . . . thing!”

“I got one that isn’t so gross,” Ella said. She held up a rock.

“That’s not a slug. It’s a rock,” Owen pointed out.

“I know!” Ella replied. “But there’s no way I’m touching one of those icky slug things.”

“Boys: one! Girls: zee-e-ro!” said Glitter Star. He struck a very heroic pose and raised his horn high into the air.

“Team Dynamic Dragicorn smells like victory and stinky slugs!” Owen said.

4

DRAGONS ON THE RUN

"Let the second challenge begin!" Sparkle Pop proclaimed. "Victory shall be ours."

"Is it to see who gives the best unicorn rides?" Owen asked, trying to pull the gross slugs off his wings.

“Not a chance,” Sparkle Pop replied.

“It’s going to be a race,” Ella said. “But it’s over a course that will require both skill *and* speed.”

“And that’s why we’ll win,” Sparkle Pop declared. She used her rainbow-sparkled horn to point out the race track to the other three. “First, we jump over the Rotten Swamp Log, then we go past the Rock Pile of Danger through the Nightmare Forest with the Itchy Grassweeds, then across the Angry Bumpkin Bridge, and then to the finish line at the Stump of Ending.” Sparkle Pop pointed to a tall tree stump that had been split by lightning.

"Just like I planned!" he said, although no one was listening.

The group ran past the Rock Pile of Danger and hurried through the Nightmare Forest with the Itchy Grassweeds.

"Oh no!" Ella cried out. "I touched one and now I'm itchy!" Ella slowed down, scratching at her scales. Sparkle Pop galloped past her.

Glitter Star quickly pranced through the Itchy Grassweeds, trying not to touch any. "Whoops!" Glitter Star said as he ran into a large, itchy pile. "I hope my legs don't get a rash!"

Racing out of the forest, Sparkle Pop was still in the lead, but now Ella was in second place, followed by Owen. Glitter Star was in last place. His body shivered with itchiness. "Argh! I'm getting very itchy all of a sudden!"

But Glitter Star made his move as they raced toward the Angry Bumpkin Bridge. His hooves clattered on the bridge so loudly that it sounded like a drum. He ran past Ella and Owen, who followed closely behind. The dragon twins' feet stomped across the bridge like a hundred ogres' clubs pounding rocks into pebbles.

A voice cried out from under the bridge. "Hey! What madness is this?" A Bridge Bumpkin ran out, waving a wooden spoon and screaming angrily. Bridge Bumpkins are troll cousins known for their long, fiery red hair and short tempers. This one was dressed in pants made from old leaves and shoes made out of tree bark. His long hair flowed behind him as he ran. "If you want to cross, you owe me three squirrel nests and a heart-shaped rock to put in my organic bridge stew!"

Owen was the first to spy the Bridge Bumpkin now running after them. "We've got trouble," he called out.

"Unicorn powers activate!" Glitter Star said.

"We don't have unicorn powers to activate unless you want to make a rainbow for him!" Sparkle Pop said. "Just run like crazy!"

The contestants picked up their pace toward the finish line.

Owen raced ahead of everyone, but a few gross slugs were still stuck to him. As he gained speed, the slugs fell from his scales and plopped onto the ground in front of Glitter Star, leaving a gross slime trail.

SQUISH!

Glitter Star stepped into the slime and his hooves slipped out from under him.

"Oh no!" Owen cried when he saw his teammate wobbling. Owen slowed down but then Glitter Star crashed into him and they tumbled and slid together across the ground, stopping just short of the Stump of Ending.

Sparkle Pop and Ella crossed the finish line easily.

"Boys: one! Girls: one!" Ella said proudly. "We're tied now!"

The Bridge Bumpkin leaped to the top of the stump. He was wheezing and out of breath. He was also laughing. "That was the funniest thing I've ever seen." He waved the wooden spoon at them. "I'll accept that as payment for crossing my bridge!"

5

CRASHING DEFEAT

"Team Dynamic Dragicorn gets to choose the next challenge!" Owen excitedly flapped his wings.

"And do not say unicorn rides!" Ella said.

That's exactly what Owen was going to say, so he wiggled his nose and thought of a better idea.

"I know! Let's see who can tell the best joke!" Owen said. "Okay, so what's a unicorn's favorite food? *Unicorn on the cob!* Get it?!"

The others stared at Owen in silence.

"Your brother is so uni*corny*." Sparkle Pop sighed.

"Let's see who can do the best stunts . . . in the air!" Ella suggested.

"Uh, unicorns can't fly," Glitter Star responded.

"That's why Owen and I will have to carry you," Ella explained.

"Lucky me," Glitter Star said with a groan.

"I've always dreamed of soaring through the fluffy, soft rainclouds and seeing what's on the tops of trees!" An eager Sparkle Pop scraped a hoof on the ground.

"Then let's show these boys how it's done!" Ella cheered.

Ella gently grabbed Sparkle Pop with her claws and rolled her into her arms. They zoomed away up into the sky!

"WAAAAA-HOOOOOOOOOO!" Sparkle Pop shouted. "This is better than a jelly bean rainbow!"

Ella flapped her wings as fast as she could and flew into a loop-de-loop directly over Owen and Glitter Star.

"W-we're not gonna do *that*, are we?!" Glitter Star felt like his horn was wilting.

"Uh-uh. No way!" Owen said.

Ella and Sparkle Pop shot across the sky, diving, spinning, banking, and twirling, happily laughing like two dwarves in a mud puddle.

ZIP! WHIZZ! SHOOM!

Ella banked to the left. She folded her wings and dove straight for Owen and Glitter Star.

"She's gonna crash!" Glitter Star panicked.

"She's a *dragon*," Owen huffed. "Dragons *don't* crash."

Ella opened her wings at the last second.

FOOM!

Ella and Sparkle Pop made a perfect dragon landing right in front of Owen and Glitter Star.

"YAWN!" Owen greeted them.

"Top that, Bro," Ella said with a chuckle.

"Our turn!" Owen said to Glitter Star. "Get ready to kick some dragon tail *and* unicorn horn."

Owen flapped his wings, scooped up Glitter Star, and shot into the sky.

"YAAAAAAAAHHH!" Glitter Star screamed. "I don't think I like being a flying unicorn!"

"Get ready for a loop!" Owen said.

"I thought you said we weren't doing a loop!" a panicked Glitter Star said.

"We're not doing *a* loop! We're doing *ten*!" Owen flapped his wings faster.

"AAAAAAAAHHH!" Glitter Star shouted. He twisted around in Owen's claws and wrapped his legs around Owen's body.

"Let go of me! I can't fly like this!" Owen shouted.

"Good! 'Cause I don't want to fly anymore!" Glitter Star whined.

Owen tried to flap his wings, but one was pinned down by Glitter Star and the two of them spiraled out of control.

"AAAAAAAAHHH!" Glitter Star shouted as they plummeted. "Crashing is way worse than flying!"

SPLASH!

Owen and Glitter Star crashed into a large mud puddle.

"Ugh! I'll never get this mud out of my mane," Glitter Star complained. "I thought you said dragons *never* crash."

"We don't!" Owen grumbled. "Unless a screaming, nutty unicorn is flying with us!"

"Oh well, boys!" Ella laughed. "Looks like it's two to one—girls are in the lead!"

6

UNDER THE RAINBOW

Ella, Owen, Sparkle Pop, and Glitter Star gathered in a clearing near the mud puddle.

"The fourth challenge will be to see who gives the best unicorn rides!" Sparkle Pop announced.

"REALLY?!" Owen gasped.

“Nah. Just kidding.” Sparkle Pop laughed.

Owen folded his wings in and puffed smoke from his nose. “Unicorns are about as funny as a two-eyed cyclops,” he grumbled.

“The fourth challenge will be . . . making a rainbow!” Sparkle Pop announced.

"We're dragons. We can't make rainbows!" Ella protested.

"Don't worry, my dragon friend," Sparkle Pop replied. "We've got this. The only thing unicorns love more than a rainbow is a rainbow that's barfing another rainbow."

"Okay, then!" Ella smiled and stepped in front of the two boys, dramatically flapping her wings.

“And now, all the way from the Lollipop Forest, put your claws and hooves together for . . . Sparkle Pop, the unicorn!” Ella called out like a master of ceremonies.

“And from wherever dragons come from . . . Ella, the dragooooon!” Sparkle Pop joined in. “Now let’s get ready to RAINBOOOOOOOOOOW! Follow my lead, teammate. . . .”

Sparkle Pop started the "rainbow dance" and pranced to the left. Then she bent her knees and wiggled her tail.

"NEIGH! NEIGH!"

Ella did the same.

"Uh . . . neigh, neigh?"

Sparkle Pop pranced to the right, bent her knees, and wiggled her tail again.

"NEIGH! NEIGH!"

Ella followed along. "Neigh again! And, um, neigh some more!"

Sparkle Pop swiveled her body and called out, “By the magicks given to all unicorns by the Caramel Queen under the twelfth rising of the Licorice Moon, I call forth the powers of Roy G. Biv, Painter of Skies!”

“Yeah! What she said!” Ella shouted and blew fire into the air.

Sparkle Pop's horn glowed red, then orange, yellow, green, blue, indigo, and finally violet.

SHOOM!

A kaleidoscope of glittering colors burst from Sparkle Pop's horn and arced across the sky, making the most beautiful rainbow Ella had ever seen in her life.

"WHOOOAAAAA!" Ella gasped. "That's even more amazing than a dragon's fire tornado!"

Suddenly, Ella's tail began to shake and glow.

"Am I gonna make a rainbow too?!" Ella gasped with delight.

Ella's tail glowed red, then orange, yellow, green, blue, indigo, and finally violet.

GLOOP!

Instead of a rainbow shooting out from her tail, a gooey mess of colors slopped forth and covered her in rainbow "paint."

"I guess this is what happens when you're not a unicorn and you do the rainbow dance," Ella said as the colors dripped off her scales.

"Nice try, Sis!" Owen laughed.

"Let's see you do better, scales for brains!" Ella sneered.

"I don't have to, 'cause Glitter Star already did," Owen said. "*His* rainbow looks a little bit different than Sparkle Pop's. And by different, I mean TEAM DYNAMIC DRAGICORN AWESOME!!!"

Ella and Sparkle Pop looked up at the sky and what they saw made Ella's scales sag and Sparkle Pop's mane curl.

Glitter Star's rainbow didn't just arc across the sky, it twisted and turned and looped and spiraled and made shapes Ella didn't even know rainbows could make. Cheering gnomes slid down the rainbow like it was a waterslide.

A joyful Owen blew smoke circles around Ella's scowling face. "Oooo! Put that on your tail and wag it!" Owen laughed.

Ella blew fire, trying to scorch Owen's tail, but missed.

"Sorry, girls!" Glitter Star said with a chuckle. "Team Dynamic Dragicorn won the rainbow challenge, so the boys just tied the score, two to two!"

"Looks like we need a tiebreaker," Sparkle Pop said.

7
THE TIEBREAKER

"This is the worst idea ever," Owen whispered.

"Maybe we should just call it a tie?" Sparkle Pop whispered back.

"Whose idea w-w-was this, anyway?" a frightened Glitter Star stammered.

"Yours!" Ella replied.

With the score tied two to two, no one had been able to think of a challenge to prove once and for all who was better, girls or boys. Then Glitter Star had suggested they see who can tickle a storm giant and make him laugh first.

And so they found themselves huddled behind a huge rock near the top of Thunder Mountain watching a storm giant sharpen his lightning bolts nearby. Thunder Mountain was nothing but gray, hard stone with no plants in sight. Dark clouds filled the sky overhead, waiting for the storm giant to unleash his fury on the world below.

The storm giant was made of granite and stood over sixty feet tall. He had gray eyes and a long, gray stone beard. This one's name was Grimgar the Thunderer and his job was to create the loudest thunderstorms possible.

"Remind me to remind you to never listen to my ideas again," Glitter Star said, whimpering to Owen.

"You guys can always quit and just admit we're the best," Ella said.

"I'd rather be stuck to the bottom of a storm giant's stinky foot for the next billion years than quit!" Owen said. His fear was suddenly replaced by annoyance at the thought of losing to his sister.

Grimgar the Thunderer hammered away at his mighty lightning bolt and the mountain trembled.

"Listen, Bro, if this doesn't work out and we end up at the end of a lightning bolt, there's just, ah . . . something I've gotta tell you. . . ." Ella began.

"Yeah, Sis?" Owen said, feeling the tug of brotherly love in his dragon heart.

"GIRLS ARE BETTER THAN BOYS!!!" Ella yelled and stuck out her tongue as she raced toward Grimgar the Thunderer.

Owen scrambled after Ella while Sparkle Pop and Glitter Star hung back.

"Dragons sure are crazier than unicorns," Sparkle Pop said.

"At least those two dragons are," Glitter Star agreed.

Ella and Owen raced up to Grimgar the Thunderer's enormous feet.

"Tickle! Tickle! Tickle!" Ella and Owen both said as if they were playing with a baby ogre's tiny feet instead of a giant's fully grown and humongous feet.

"HA! HA! HA! HA! HA!"

Grimgar the Thunderer laughed so loud, the mountain shook. **"HA! HA! HA! HA! HA!"** echoed through the valley far below, rattling cottages and dungeons alike.

"I did it! The girls won!" Ella yelled.

"I tickled him first!" Owen countered.

"No, I did!" Ella replied.

"I did!"

"I did!"

"HA! HA! HA! HA!" Grimgar the Thunderer was laughing so hard that he dropped one of his lightning bolts.

"This isn't going to end well, is it?" Ella asked as the lightning bolt was about to crash down on top of them.

"RUN AWAY!" Owen yelled. Ella and Owen ran toward Sparkle Pop and Glitter Star, but it was too late. The lightning bolt hit the mountainside.

BLA-BLA-BOOOOOOM!

There was a huge explosion followed by an avalanche of rocks that rumbled toward Ella, Owen, and the unicorns.

"Oopsie," Grimgar the Thunderer said as he stopped laughing. He hoped no one would notice the mess he had just made.

8

ROCKS AND ROLLS

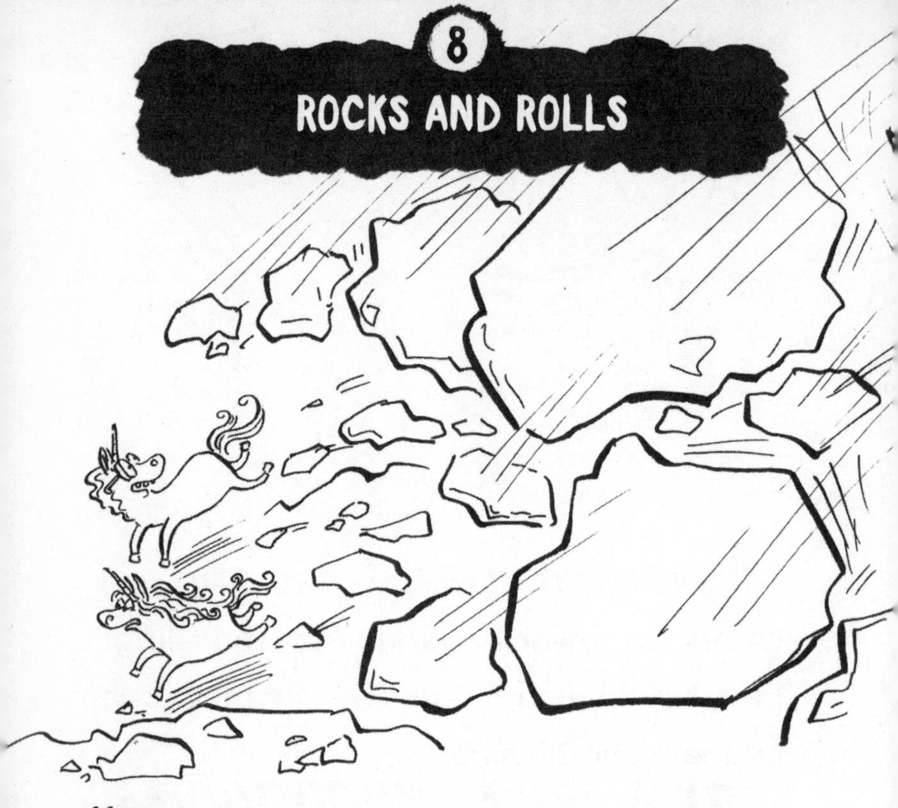

"RUN AWAY SOME MORE!" Owen shouted.

He and Ella flapped their wings and flew into the air.

"Whew! That was close!" Owen sighed.

"Wait . . . I just remembered something very important," Ella said.

"That storm giants are clumsy as heck?" Owen asked.

"No! UNICORNS CAN'T FLY!" Ella gasped.

"AAAAAAAAAAAAAAAH!"

Sparkle Pop and Glitter Star screamed from the valley below as they tried to run from the avalanche.

"AAAAAAAAAAAAAAAH!"

Ella and Owen shouted back at them.

Boulders the size of an ogre's big belly tumbled toward Sparkle Pop and Glitter Star. Just as they were about to be flattened into unicorn pancakes, Ella and Owen swooped down and lifted the two unicorn twins up into the sky.

"I never thought I'd be so happy to fly again! THANK YOU!" Glitter Star said to Owen.

"Aw, dragon scales! We're not out of trouble yet!" Owen said. "Look!"

The tumbling rocks crashed into one of the ends of Glitter Star's rainbow at the bottom of Thunder Mountain. The rainbow shattered like candy-colored glass. The twisting, turning, rollercoaster rainbow began to fall apart . . . with some gnomes still on it!

"What are we gonna do?!" Ella cried. "They're gonna fall and we can't catch them all!"

"We've gotta do another rainbow dance!" Sparkle Pop called out to Glitter Star.

"I'm on it!" Glitter Star said. "Ella! Owen! No time to land, so do what I say and let's hope this works! FLY LEFT!"

Ella and Owen flew to the left, the unicorns still in their arms. Sparkle Pop and Glitter Star pranced their legs in the air.

"NEIGH! NEIGH!"

"FLY RIGHT!" Sparkle Pop called out.

Ella and Owen turned to the right. Sparkle Pop and Glitter Star pranced their legs in the air once again.

"NEIGH! NEIGH!"

The rainbow continued to break apart. The gnomes held on with their little gnome hands, trying to not fall off.

"REAR BACK!" Glitter Star called out.

The dragons reared back and the unicorns kicked their front legs into the air. "By the magicks given to all unicorns by the Caramel Queen under the twelfth rising of the Licorice Moon, I call forth the powers of Roy G. Biv, Painter of Skies!" Sparkle Pop and Glitter Star shouted.

SHOOM! SHOOM!

Twin rainbows burst forth from Sparkle Pop's and Glitter Star's horns and shot toward the gnomes just as the last remaining parts of the broken rainbow shattered into small pieces. The gnomes landed on the new rainbows and safely slid to the ground.

"Wa-hooooo! That was the best ride ever!" one of the gnomes cheered and high-fived his brother.

9
LET'S RIDE

"Okay, since we're still tied, the *next* tiebreaker is to see who can ride on the back of a ten-headed Hydra," Ella said.

"But Hydras bite!" Owen replied.

"Not *all* their heads bite," Ella reminded him. "Some of them just spit burning acid instead."

"Do we really need another tiebreaker?" Glitter Star blew his long mane out from his eyes. "I mean, look how great it was when we all worked together to save those gnomes."

"And we'd probably be digging our way out from underneath that avalanche if it weren't for both of you," Sparkle Pop said to Ella and Owen.

"Well, we couldn't have saved those gnomes without you guys," Owen replied.

"You're right, Glitter Star, the four of us *do* make a great team," Ella agreed. "Girls and, uh, well, boys. Even my brother."

"So let's hear it for Team Rainbow and the Daring Dragons!" Owen said.

"How about let's hear it for a new name?" Ella said.

"Team Dragon Force and the Universal Unicorns?" Owen answered.

"Nope," Ella replied.

"We may not be able to agree on a name, but one thing we *can* agree on is that boys and girls are *both* awesome!" Sparkle Pop cheered.

"Although twin dragons *are* better than twin unicorns," Ella whispered to Owen.

"Although twin unicorns *are* better than twin dragons," Sparkle Pop whispered to Glitter Star.

Glitter Star reared back on his hind legs and let out a majestic neigh.

"And now, to celebrate our awesomeness . . . and the fact that Owen will finally stop coming up with lame names . . ." Glitter Star began.

"Team Draco Fire Wing Stompers and the Ultimate Unicornificent Unicorns?" Owen tried one last time.

". . . It's time for some unicorn rides!" Glitter Star finished.

“This is the best day ever!” Owen said, smacking his tail on the ground with excitement.

“Especially since I didn’t end up stuck to the bottom of a storm giant’s stinky foot,” Ella agreed.

The rest of the day was filled with unicorn rides and rainbow slides. From the ground under their claws to the fluffy clouds in the sky, there was never a better day for two dragons and their two new friends.

"I can't believe it, Owen," Ella said. "I thought today would be full of arguments and unhappiness, but it really turned out to be the greatest day ever!"

"I know!" Owen replied. "It doesn't matter if you have wings, a horn, or ten heads that spit burning acid, you can still be my friend!"

As the sun set and the unicorn rainbows faded, Ella and Owen said goodbye to their new friends.

"You're welcome to come visit our cave any time," Ella said.

"And we hope you'll come see us sometime in the Lollipop Forest," Sparkle Pop replied.

Ella and Owen flapped their wings and took off.

"I finally thought of a team name!" Owen said. "Team Super Scales and the Main Manes!"

"Ick! Try again," Ella said.

"Superpower Dragon Owen and His Sidekicks?" Owen said.

"On second thought, *don't* try again," Ella said as they flew toward home.

But little did they know what waited for them back at their cave. . . .

Read on for a sneak peek from the
eighth book in the Ella and Owen series.

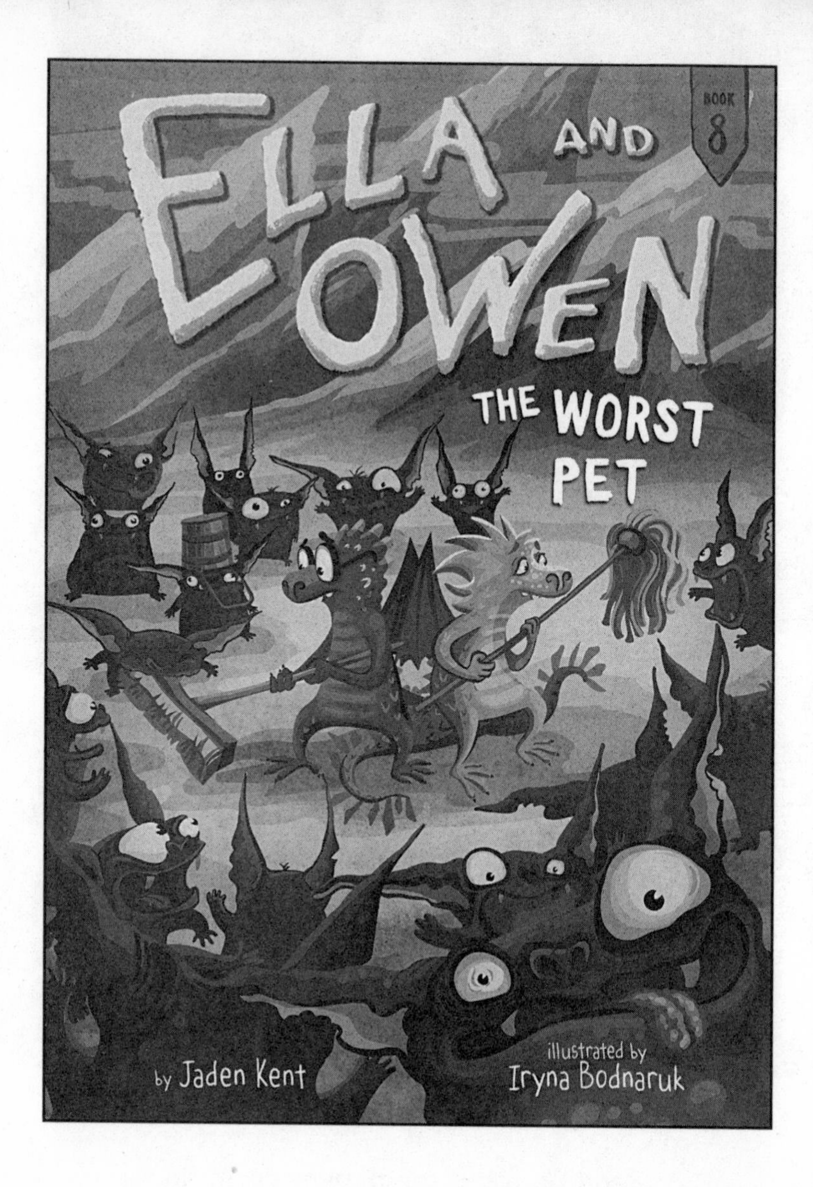
BOOK
8
ELLA AND OWEN
THE WORST PET
by Jaden Kent
illustrated by
Iryna Bodnaruk

1

SURPRISE?

"I can't believe I met a unicorn—no, TWO unicorns!" Owen twirled about excitedly in the air as he flew with his twin sister. They passed the Gumdrop Volcano, flew over the Lake of Doom, and through the Valley of Things We Don't Want to Know About. They were on their way home.

"Well, I—" Ella began.

"And they gave me a ride!" Owen could barely contain his joy.

"That was—" Ella started.

"I already miss Sparkle Pop and Glitter Star so much," Owen said with a sigh. "Don't you? They are the best unicorns with the best unicorn names ever, right? They're so . . . so . . . unicorny!"

"I liked—" Ella tried again.

"And the riding!" Owen said. "Did I mention I loved riding a unicorn?"

"More than once. You know, I—wait!" Ella stopped and sniffed the air. "Do you smell that?"

"Oh! Is it a unicorn?!" Owen's eyes lit up.

"Of course not," Ella said. "Smell for yourself."

Owen took a big sniff. "I know that smell! That's bat squid covered in onions, acorns, and snail slime."

"DINNER!" Owen and Ella shouted

at the same time.

The two dragons flew over one last hill and past the last tree in the forest before their home. They could see their family's cave close by. They landed just outside of it, and Ella cried out, "Mom! Dad!"

Their parents, Daryl and Goldenrod, flew out from the cave toward their children, nervously looking back over their wings.

"Owen! Ella! You're home!" their mom said.

"And not a minute too soon!" their dad added. "I'm still waiting for the stinky fish cake you promised me."

Owen shuffled his toe claws in

the ground. “Yeah, about that . . .” he started to say.

“Never mind,” their dad said. “Your mom’s made a lovely bat squid dinner with a fresh loaf of sourdough bread stuffed with raven’s feet.”

“We could smell it from over the hill,” Owen said. “Delicious!”

“We also have another surprise for you,” their mom added.

“Is it a jar of scale-cleansing bubble bath?” Ella asked.

“A new cushion for my reading chair?” Owen asked.

“Um . . . better,” their mom replied.

“We wanted to surprise you with . . . pets,” their dad announced.

"PETS?!" Owen exclaimed.

"Are they snaggletoothed fire goats?" Ella smacked her tail against the ground like she always did when she was excited.

"Or sidewinder rattlebugs?" Owen asked.

"I think the best thing to do would be—" their mom said, looking nervously at their dad.

"To show you," he finished.

Ella and Owen quickly followed their parents into the cave.

SMASH!

Plates and cups flew through the air.

CRASH!

The kitchen table was thrown upside down.

BASH!

Two small gremlins sat on a broken chair in the kitchen. Some pieces of the chair had crumbled to the floor. One gremlin was bashing pots and pans together while the other ate a large candle like it was corn on the cob. Broken dishes were scattered across the kitchen floor.

The gremlins had short, thin arms and legs and pot bellies and were covered in green scales. They had large noses and pointy ears that perked up when they saw Ella and Owen.

"And . . . well . . . here they are," Ella and Owen's dad said, cracking a weak smile.

The twins stared at the gremlins.

"Are the new pets behind the gremlins?" Owen asked.

"No! Your new pets are the gremlins," their dad replied.

"Surprise!" their mom added weakly.

A plate flew across the room and hit Owen in the head.

"Hehehehehehehehe!" the gremlin who'd thrown it laughed.

"Maybe next time we should just get them three-eyed goldenfish," Ella and Owen's dad whispered to their mom.